THE DOGE OF VENICE

AND OTHER STORIES

by

Duilio Chiarle

(Trad. by Antonio Siclari)

This is a work of fiction. Similarities to real people, places, or events are entirely coincidental.

THE DOGE OF VENICE AND OTHER STORIES

First edition. September 4, 2012.

Copyright © 2012 Duilio Chiarle.

ISBN: 979-8231594351

Written by Duilio Chiarle.

Table of Contents

*Devoted to all
those people I have loved
and that are not here anymore*

Some of the stories received different reviews. The whole work has got the "Città di Torino" and "Cesare Pavese" prizes.

*The Doge of Venice
and other stories*

SPEECH ON MAN

Yes, boy, I am a tramp. But not always. Do you believe someone is born willing to sleep under a bridge? Life catches you by the wrists and let you where it wants. Rummaging garbage is not so nice.

Why am I here? And who knows it. One day you are journalist, a worker, a manager. The next day you find yourself under a bridge, and you are disgusting. I am disgusting, isn't it? Yes, it is true, and you are right. I am disgusting because I don't work, because I look through the garbage, and I sleep on the benches of the park. Because I remember to the others I am here. But you have not to think, you like people watching TV: you remember them what they are. With those chains, the trimmed head. Even if you kill me, who does care? They will forget us. A nice title on someone of these newspapers I use as a blanket, and we are already yesterday's news. People want to dream, we are the nightmares. It is an old story. Me, you, people of the stadium, we are the same thing. They have not invented the stadiums have invented now at all: there have been there for three thousand years. And a reason to make war, they will always know how to give it to you.

Who am I? I have seen Troy, and I have destroyed it. I was with Solomon, I have built the Temple: I was with the Roman who set it on fire. I have crucified Jesus Christ. I have built the pyramids, the Colosseum, St.Peter's cathedral. I have besieged Jerusalem with the crusaders and when I entered, the blood licked my ankles. I have sung while Rome burnt. I have exterminated Greek people in the name of Allah. When the Huns passed, I was there. I have built the Great Wall of China. I have known Quetzalcoatl. I have seen the long knives. I have killed Sitting Bull. I have been gladiator, a kamikaze. They spread me to the beasts. I was a rapist Viking. I have exterminated the Celts. I am the one who invented the wheel. I have picked up the fire. I have founded Rome. I have invented the extermination camps. I am the man, boy, I am you.

THE DOGE OF VENICE

Yes, I know I owe my fortune to the sea, but I cannot stand it and I cannot wait to come back home. Yes, it is nice to be seen, when the Sun raises from the lagoon and I lean out the window, I look at it shining on the roofs, sparkling on the water, caressing the marbles of my town. Then I take a breath of air smelling of salt and rotten wood. The problem is that I cannot stay on a boat without feeling bad. I cannot even swim. But after all, what need would I have to swim? At the warehouse, the rare times I have gone there, I have seen only barges, boxes and barrels. It is beautiful to smell the fragrance of the perfume of spice, even if the ginger makes me sneeze. I had not been going to the warehouse for years by now. I am not younger, and I don't even need it in my position. In the morning, when I look at the Sun, I hear the cries of the boatmen: they don't bother me. I always get up very early, because early to rise makes a man healthy, and I have to deal with a lot of practices. But my sorrow is due to those hulls of walnut-tree we call "ships". I have always suffered seasickness. Going to Torcello is a torture. I hardly bear some brief journey by boat, when my servant ferries me along the channels. I don't bear the sea, it really doesn't suit me. Even now, on this expensive ship, I feel a knot in my stomach, as if one big hand grabbed and held it, it twisted it. It is a fortune that in the building there is all I need: I don't need to go around. I can go calmly to mass, on foot. Yes my father's father sailed on the ships, and he fought. I didn't, I don't like the sight of blood and I gladly leave it to others. I remember when I was a boy, I sometimes ran away along the *calles* and I mixed myself with the people, in the middle of the merchants and the fishermen selling theirs malodorous load: I liked it, once; the maidservant despaired. Poor Mary! I regret that period just because I was very young, but now I feel at my ease. Here I do what I want and nobody can order me anything. When I sit on that seat, in that enormous living room, I feel better than a king, since the ambassadors have to bow themselves. I am sat and I look at them with benevolence or with indifference, according to that their prince pleases or not to the Serene Highness. I have coldly welcomed the envoy from the Basileus. I have treated with contempt the envoys from the Pope. My benevolent eye looked at the imperial messenger. The day before yesterday, I have inflicted two death sentences; secret, of course. Today it is so, tomorrow everything could change. There are people that, in order to see me, travel for weeks. Me, the longest trip I have done, it was to Chioggia, but I don't like that place, it is not safe. Here, in the lagoon, the hostile ships would strand; who can invade Venice?

I feel bad. This fool ship is disgusting as well as those rowers over there. By luck I won't get on here this year. The sea is as very beautiful to be seen as ugly to be touched. And I don't want to stay for a long time on this crock. Last year there was a storm; just one year ago. There was a heavy "cloak" above Venice and the washing of the oars could be heard strong: a deaf and obsessive noise, like also the rowers' moans. Too slow. At the end I have gotten soaked of water and I have risked getting sick like my master of ceremonies.

Look at this idiot on my side, how he feels at his ease. And how he speaks! Just as well it is my turn: those fool men, there on the shore, they adore this useless and expensive ceremony. They are satisfied with so little... Now the idiot has ended and it is my turn. I have to stand up.

"Oh sea,
we marry you,
in sign of real
and perfect dominion!"

Here, the ring has gone. Ten gold sequins spread to the fishes. The Bucentaur has given a jolt. I cannot wait to come back home. Listen how they shout happy over there. And think how some of them starve.

I don't like sea, I cannot wait to come back home.

GRAJANO

You won't perhaps believe it, but everything started in a fool tavern. Do you know how it happens, isn't it? One drinks, the other one drinks... One boasts, the other one boasts... One man shouts and the insults fly. How can I remember the beginning of the matter? I was not even there. When Guy has insulted them, those in the tavern were eight against two. That's why he told them "cowardly men". He had perhaps exaggerated a little: he liked wine very much after all. You will wonder how it is possible that two enemies meet at the same tavern. It was winter, who could make war in winter? We besieged the Swabian caste; there were the Spanish men from Cordoba inside. I don't remember well the name of our commander... Nemours! That's how the hell his name was. Well you know how these things go. Guy says a bad word, they become very angry and some slaps fly, Guy says "Cowards, you are good only if you are so many", that other says "I can crush three of them by myself". In other words, to make it brief, the idea to make a nice tournament comes out. Thirteen against thirteen, who loses will be paying. Innkeeper! Something to drink to everybody, I will pay!

Thirteen against thirteen, I said. Good affair! However soldiers liked the idea. Thirteen Italians at Spanish men service against thirteen of the French field. By Jove! A judge by part, Bajardo to us, Prospero Colonna to them. Everybody betted on this and that and on who would have been done imprisoned for first. During a siege time never passes by, they will have to do something. It is hard to find thirteen champions nowadays. When Guy called me, he said "I give him the bet!" *"Ok"*, I answered. Then he made me see their list. Their names can be remembered by everybody, but not ours. Except for mine, of course. Being in the list it was an honour and one could even round out the salary. The man from Lodi was among them. What a good ally that one! Thinking that Lombards made us go over there. But after all it was to understand, poor Fanfulla. The pay was good and the Spaniards paid well. I didn't know the others, but I know they had fame to be smart persons. Then, innkeeper! This wine? A bet, I said. It was only a bet: who loses, he pays. I didn't think they would have talked so much about. However it was really a nice challenge. There were some good riders by us. I mention them to you, because nobody surely told you about: Guy de La Motte, Charles de Tourges, Marc de Frignes, Giraud de Forces, Martellin de Lambris, Pierre de Liaye, Jacques de La Fontaine, Eliot de Baraut, Jean de Landes, Sacet de Jacet, Jacques de Guignes, Naute de La Fraise. And I was also there.

It was a beautiful tournament, even if they competed better. Ah! The impetus of the battle, the din of the hoofs! We finally did something different than playing the dice! But it lasted very short for me, because they almost immediately broke my head. It was the year 1503; the thirteenth of a month I don't remember anymore, I think it was February. And there is someone going around saying they killed me. Instead I am alive and kicking, only sometimes amnesia comes, and I don't know what I am doing. How was it? They won: they were more capable.

Every now and then, someone asks me what happened later: nothing, the siege of Barletta continued like before. The king of Spain for them, the king of France for us.

Sometimes, when the weather is changing, my head it still hurting. What's my name? Grajan, Claude Grajan, from Asti. Let is be, my friend, I will pay.

DRINK WITH ME
PUBLIO CORNELIO SCIPIONE

My life was a battle. I was only nine years old when my father made me swear in the temple. I led to war people and tribes. What could the world expect from me? I am old and tired, and there is a garrison out there that doesn't dare to come and arrest me: they are afraid of me and you, poor men! Think they grew and matured with those scrap metals in their hands. And think today their Country dominates the sea. They won't leave stone on stone. They won't be satisfied with this victory. Conditions are hard, but as soon as my town has paid the tribute, when there is nothing else to be plundered, they will take the inhabitants away. Publio Cornelius, you are a brave man and you are ashamed of the merchandise made by your Senate. But we know the Senate of your town is the same of mine: the profit and all its perverse logic move it. But I understood this too late, since I saw my town again just before the only defeat. My Senate would have treated yours with the same contempt. Publio, did you let me free for this reason? I came back in town, and I built a new movement that destroyed the power of the merchant Senate. It was a rich town, before them. Publio, I know you agree with me: if I had won the merchants in my town, this motion would also have happened in yours. You are a stubborn, you would have tried too. But my Senate agreed with yours, and when they saw I was against their common interest, they didn't hesitate to ask my deportation. Publio, you used all your influence, in the hope to prevent the worse, and I thank you. The fool, dull mentality of the merchants had unfortunately the better of it on the purest spirits. Merchants want the war because it is worthwhile: Publio, you already knew it. We have spent our whole life in the war. Before my Senate delivered me, before the order came peremptory, you gave me the means to run away, and I thank you about. Do you remember the wound I made you in Zama? Well, does it make you laugh? Be careful Publio, they fear you in Rome as well as they feared me in Carthage.

Antioco was afraid of me too. How was he? A good sovereign, but militarily he was incapable; he moved the army on the bases of the army of Alexander from Macedonia, and he didn't realize such an army was good one century before, when his great-great-grandfather took possession of the kingdom of Syria. Then, this people don't feel like fighting because too rich, and who lives in the luxury, they don't feel like risking their life; men that have nothing to lose, they risk. But when it was the moment to make war, he wanted to command the army in person: with you in front of him, all the men of the kingdom would not have been enough for him. He lined up a banal army... In Magnesia he lost the war in just one battle. Publio, I went away from Antioch with the *etolo* Toante.

But I was the danger. I was inciting people against the merchant senates. Everywhere I went, everyone tried to sell themselves. I got tired. I have sixty seven years old, and I spent all of them in war. Someone else will think about the merchants. My town will be destroyed, but only when the rich people have saved all. And we have destroyed half world for this reason.

Your legionaries are out there, but they don't dare to come in. And you, Publio Cornelius Scipio, what are you waiting for? You know I won't go to Rome to let they torture me. For this reason I want to toast with you with this wine. Take this cup, Publio, it is good wine: the poison is in mine.

Let's give the calm back to the Romans, considering they have not the patience to wait for the end of an old man like me.

Drink with me, Publio, with this sentence I have satisfied the posterity.

THE LEFT-HANDED

What are you saying, innkeeper? Have I drunk too much? And would you tell me I drink too much? I am one person who works, even if I have only one hand. My name is Caio Muzio Cordo, but everyone calls me "*Scevola*" that means left-handed. This by the Republic. It is a long story, my goodness. Have I lost my right hand, do you know how? No, I have not lost it in battle, even if they tell so. No, I have lost it in the hostile field, but not in battle.

When have thrown out the Tarquinis from Rome, and these have escaped to Chiusi, the senatorial Fathers proclaimed the Republic. Gods know what it means. At least they said so, I don't know it, and I am a shepherd. There was then the war with Tyrrhenian people, those from Chiusi. There was a king called Porsenna, and they said he was the more powerful person in the world. You live in town, and it is all right to you, war or not, it doesn't change anything. But I live in country and all those soldiers threatened my livestock. Those dotards sat to discuss and talk, while Tyrrhenian people plundered the fields. And then I thought "If I kill him, war will be over". And since I speak Etruscan, I go to the hostile field and I kill Porsenna. I thought: "If he is a king, he will be well dressed, important, respected by everyone".

Coming into the field, it was easy. What do you say? No, it is not a lie; I seriously went in the field. And here I see my man, the one wearing those beautiful clothes, making some signs on a table. I went behind him, pretending nothing and... Zac! The drove the dagger in his back. But he was another man, not Porsenna. So they arrested me and brought in front of the king. He had a severe face and he was very fat, he didn't look like a king at all. I said to him "It was you that I wanted to kill, not the other one". He realized I said the truth. I knew well what I expect: a capital punishment, used as example. So I thought about making a beautiful scene. I said to him "My hand was wrong and I now punish it" and I have thrust my right hand in the brazier. I had nothing to lose. Know, innkeeper, that arm of mine was insensitive since I was a child, when I had an accident, with the ox... So I didn't feel anything. But people, there inside, got impressed very much, also because I have not made a single grimace. Then Porsenna got up and said *"It's enough! Men like this don't deserve the death!"* I don't remember very well then, but when I wake up, I was in our field. It was good, I saved my skin, I was home again and everybody honoured me. That hand of mine was always useless, paralytic as it was. I am left-handed, I was always left-handed. What a fortune! Don't you believe it innkeeper? Have you not ever heard about me? I am Muzio, Muzio the left-handed, everyone knows me here... Give me some drops more...

THE OUTLET
OF THE DEACON PAUL

<< I don't know if these few lines of mine will arouse the curiosity of the posterity. I don't know if they will outlive in the centuries... (illegible passage)...

I have been preceptor of Adelperga, Desiderio's daughter, the lamented sovereign of the Longobards. I myself am Longobard, proud child of this obstinate race, and servant of the father of all the creatures of the world. Now, everything about my friends is cancelled. What remained about Roman spirit is cancelled. The Lombard memory fades away; the suburbs disappear for the joy of the division of the loot. Ransacking the houses, the fields, the cemeteries. When Pavia was taken, I thought "The Franks have won: therefore, they will bring everything away." It is true, they brought away the gold and iron, as my ancestors did to the Goths that did it to the Romans, which plundered Gallics, Greeks and Etrurians. But the gentlemen, those important, remained at their place.

My reader, you that are reading these lines, reflect on the frailty of the man! Who commands today, he is dust tomorrow. Who is arrogant today, tomorrow he prostrates and asks for payment. This way it is for every sovereign dynasty, so it is for everybody. Also the Franks are prostrating one day. Even the Basileus.

The ancients erected monuments. The trace left by the sovereigns, the general, the senators, the noble remains in the history. Seven the wonders of the world are. But who built the wonders? Someone speaks of the servant that was killed by his master, someone tells about the farmer that set the first stone of the tower of Babel; who carved the head of the Colossus of Rhodes? How would have made the great Caesar without the legionaries? And what would have done Carlo Martello without his riders at Poitiers?

I am old. I am almost eighty years old. Also the king of the Franks has honoured me, since I know the magic of the writing, and I read without telling a word. About Desiderio, he was a good king. He was too good king to stay for a long time. In a kingdom, the king doesn't command, but his barons. And the barons, after the defeat, have remained at their place. And even this duke from Benevento, now so proud: where was he when the enemy passed S. Michael's locks? He was in his court, worried that his hens made more eggs; bothered by the supplications of his concubines and by the noise of the bastard children singing in the courtyard. Where were the barons, when Charles the Frank played the Oliphant?

I know where they were: to supervise their fortitudes, built by the servants. A master is like the other to them. So, please let therefore the bitterness of an old deacon has outlet and flows like a stream after the summer storm. The servants remained servants; the masters are always the same: what is changed therefore? And will it perhaps change anything, if the Saracens will come?>>

(And here, the Master's parchment interrupts.)

WHAT ARE YOU SAYING STUPID MAN?

What are you saying stupid man? Do you realize you are wrong? Didn't your mother explain you how universe works? Don't you listen to the sermon on Sundays?

I always have been tilling the soil, and I have never seen it was different. You want to cheat me! Be careful! Even if your dress is made of elegant cloth, even if you have the power to read the signs of the quill pen, I cannot believe this lie of yours. I am on this land where the father of father's father already worked in the fields. I don't speak as well as you. I don't know what moves the seasons. I know there is a time for the seeding and one for the crop. I know spring comes and all blooms. And then the summer is here and we make the bonfires in that night. And then the autumn comes and the leaves fall down, and the cold comes. And in the night in November we put the chestnuts out of the door because the souls return and they want to eat. And in winter there is the snow and God's creatures sleep and rest. The first day of January we lean our ear on the ground to listen to the noises, and if we hear the noise of a wagon we know that it is bad sign and that year there will be a poor crop. In winter, in the evening people gather in Bodo's stall, now Groldo's one, sometimes at Mentone's; close to the fire, my people tell the ancient stories. It will be, but I have never heard the story you tell me, I don't believe it. You make fun of me because I am a farmer and I work the land. I have so many seasons on this head hardened by the sun, on this back bent by the hoe. You cannot make fun of me this way. I am a free man, I am Christian, and I am older than you. And I will never believe in this thing you tell me: earth cannot be round. Men would fall out from there. You cannot make fun of me. I am older...

THE HUNTER

It is easy to shoot the bucks. All it takes is forgetting they are bucks, and you shoot. That's all. It is very easy by my crossbow. A touch, a hiss... Even agony is little, if you can aim well. However, hunting is dangerous. And then it is forbidden to hunt the bucks. Only to the king it is allowed. Nevertheless, there are many poachers.

I am one who know his job. I don't like to violate laws. They arrest you for nothing, and you don't go out anymore. Once I have seen a cell made of stone; the prisoner was there, stretched out on a bench. Under the bench, there was a grating from which the air came in. They told me that nobody lived more than one month in that place. Thinking about it, I have a shiver. This can always happen in my job. Shooting to a man is dangerous, but not so much hunting the king's bucks. In this Country, it is even a cult. This people love as much their king as they love to challenge his laws; such people can have only a nobility of opposite tendency: they respect laws and don't love their king.

Here they are, riding the horse. Just like they told me. Just as well, the rope was already tight, and it could let go. Let's see now... The one holding the shield with the lion... The one over there. Well, he is coming. Now... Go! Ah! I have hit him... Damn! I have hit him on his shoulder... It doesn't matter, the arrow was poisoned. I have a long head... Look at those ones running. Don't I care if that one is a duke or King Richard? Tomorrow, another one commands, and I will be rich. It is better

I reload my crossbow. Who knows? I don't trust these three men...

THE GRENADIER

I respect your decisions, my son. Yours, it is a noble gesture. I also left instead of another person that was the only son, and I got grenadier. I was in captain Bozzolino's department.

There was a terrible war, one of those that you don't know why they start. One day we moved here, one day there. Sometimes one shot. The grenadiers shoot a little, because they have to put the mine. Don't know what it is? It is better for you, my son. Put a log that your mother is cold. Therefore, I said, there was a terrible war that nobody understood the reason why. And we were losing; I believe. Well, however, we were inside a fortitude in Turin. They called it "the citadel". It was like many bunkers put around the town. I have never seen anything stranger. You should have seen them! They were so many! Lined by flags, and in front of every flag, there was a well-dressed officer with his shiny sword. They remained in that position for a long time. It was a show to take the breath away. At that moment, it was also nice to be seen. Then the gun burst, because sometimes it happens. After some time, they arrived from everywhere. More than flies. We as sappers have been recalled back. The others have almost been all massacred. There were the officers, and you can read the defeat on their faces. They already saw the sacking, the rapes. Instead, a group of ours came back and threw them out. They didn't expect it. Then the general of French people, he asked a truce to bring away the wounded persons, to remove the corpses. However, our general told him he would have cared about them... There will have been at least three thousand people out there. In the ditch, there were people asking for help: ours and theirs. Who distinguished them? My son, if it happens to you to go to war, know that wounded persons are the same. The general made us throw in the ditch so many faggots and then... He made to set fire. There were a lot of people howling; the general laughed. I don't like to tell these things. I never told them. It is better I drink something. Forgive me, my son.

As French people were good and waited for that fire stopped, we as sappers have been sent for few days to the Aid Demilune. Don't look at me this way, my son. I didn't call it this way. They were afraid that someone entered the citadel from the undergrounds, and then they made us prepare a stove of emergency in the connection staircase between the two galleries: tall and low. By chance, the enemies discovered the door of the tall gallery. Then we prepared the mine. It was a big job: there were some barrels of dust and a long fuse. We mounted guard in turn, because if French people entered, we would have had to set the powder on fire. Nevertheless, nobody believed seriously that they would have reached the stove. I was a guard, with my companion from Sagliano. We immediately realized that something was wrong. There was a noise, out there. In fact, four French persons with the caress, they went down with the ropes, and someone started shooting. Then others arrived. My friend realized that French people were winning, so he barred the access. Meanwhile, I tried to connect the fuse, because I had the time. At a certain point, we heard the dull thuds: French people won and they were entering. They were breaking the front door with their axes. "Hurry up" he said to me *"Hurry up!"* However, I realized the fuse was not good, and I wanted to take another one.

"Get away" he said, *"you are very slow...."* He took the fuse and put it in the stove. I gave the torch to him, and I ran away. He lighted, and immediately followed me. After ten steps, the mine already burst, while French people opened the front door. However, the mine had to burst later; it was a long fuse. I realized that it didn't work.

When the mine burst, I felt myself lift like a branch of acacia. I got up from the ground with a terrible ache in my bones. *"Peter!"* I called him. *"Peter!"* Behind a heap of rubble, I have heard someone having the death rattle. He was behind there. *"I take you away!"* I said to him. "Don't worry, I take you away!." He looked me. I tried to lift him, but he howled. Then a rifleman arrived and helped me to take him out. He died after a long time, and I cried, because I knew that he had a family. That's how Peter Micca has gone. I have told the captain the fuse burnt too fast and he told it the general. If I was silent, they would have given me a prize. They put me in the front line again. It was August 29th 1706. They gave one pay day to his widow. Put a log in the fireplace, my son, your mother is cold.

THE EMPEROR'S SOLDIERS

My God, I never saw a department more disciplined. Thirty soldiers, two hoers, a lance-corporal, a sergeant and a drummer. Impeccable, in their blue watch uniform, they seemed to come from nothing. They were times in which the brigands were shed everywhere, they multiplied their teams every day. One particularly terrorized whole countries and towns. They told with one only ball, he killed five soldiers and a horse; he was tall more than two meters, that he lifted a barrel of wine above his own head, that he hit a fly one hundred feet far by his gun. All lies, of course. However, the only idea that Maynos was circulating, it made the presence of French soldiers more pleasant. Mayno, at least, could keep them busy and not to give them the time to rape, sack and some other activities which the soldiers are often devoted in dark times. Therefore, seeing those soldiers so unusually disciplined, with that impeccable officer to march perfectly under the sun of July, it made me forget the danger of the brigands. The men were sweaty, but tidy. The time of march was articulated by the drum. A dry sound like the fields in summer. *"Citizen" the officer said to me "You won't have boredom from my soldiers."* They just didn't feel at their ease wearing those black hats. I looked at them; some were very young, others looked at some fathers of a family torn from their own land to be sent to a foreign country. *"We are bound to Spain"* the officer said. So impaled and silent, under the sun, they were painful. I said they could protect themselves, rather; they had to and that with this sun, it was not good to start off. *"There is still a long way to go" the officer said stretching "We need the aid box, provisions and shoes for the journey."* No, no, first they would have had a stop. Water, lodging and comfort for everybody. They would have left later in the morning, at daybreak, when the sun doesn't burn the skin. *"The country is a severe god" the officer said, "but you are right, citizen. I will accept your offer."* This way, he gave the permission to break the lines. They settled down on a pair of barns with the recommendation not to smoke. Oddly, nobody infringed. It should be a really special department; I thought. I gave hospitality to the officer in my house, and I gave disposition that all his requests were granted. It existed, at that time, a circular that imposed to the mayors to put at disposal of the military departments some high sum of money of the State and other material, and to deliver it by request, under the commander's receipt. This way, he spent the evening beating me at chess, game by game. *"You are a good player, citizen" telling the truth I had no big possibilities to make games in that country. The visitors were rare.* There was nothing better than a talk, one smoke, a glass of wine and a chess game to cheer the mantle of monotony of the Piedmontese country. And my guests often were beaten. Nevertheless, that officer was the strongest player whom I had ever met. I spent a nice evening, telling stories about brigands. I don't see them anymore, but at that time, they were common ones, source of gossip and legend. The officer had a good time and told me some Mayno's adventures that I didn't know yet, perhaps because popular imagination had not distorted the facts yet. They know, a cat passing mouth by mouth; it becomes a lion. I spent a delicious evening. The officer was a person of world, good talker, intelligent and qualified in his work. About the soldiers, they didn't make drunk; they didn't run after underskirts, they didn't steal chickens. They spent the evening playing cards. I felt sincere sorrow, the morning later, when they left. At dawn, they were already standing at attention. I delivered them thirty six pairs of shoes, provisions for five days and two thousand francs. Few orders were enough to start marching. The drum rolled, and they started marching. Who knows, if they had still transited around, we could play some game again. I don't easily resign myself to lose. *"Everyone loses, sooner or later"* the officer said, giving me the receipt. *"Sooner or later you have your revenge, my citizen".* He smiled, mounted and he went in front of the line. The drum rolled and the soldiers, all perfectly synchronized, started marching. At the first lights of the morning, on the road, they looked like the single parts of a millipede that always repeated the same synchronous movement. The officer turned and waved his hat as a sign of regard. They were out soon of sight. They had not given the least trouble.

Those that came the following day, they were not made from the same mould. They arrived in the afternoon. They were dirty and behaved like beasts. As first thing, they asked me the whole cash at disposal, food and some women. The officer, cursing, entered my house, and he used my sideboard without asking. They should be Mayno's brigands. The officer told that sometimes they used to disguise themselves as soldiers. Ah, if there were still in the country those good soldiers... I secretly sent a boy in town, by horse, asking for a detachment of lancers. Before evening, a regiment surrounded the country, and they captured them all. We verified so that they were real soldiers, but they were not at all like those of the previous day. It should be great if all emperor's soldiers were so. Clean, tidy, well-trained and obedient. Then the colonel wanted to know everything about them, who was that good officer and which department was. I delivered him the receipt of the day before, which I still held in my pocket. Little by little he kept on reading, the colonel's face got an expression of great amazement. He folded up the receipt in four parts, and he snickered. *"The best soldiers of the emperor"* he said with exaggerated emphasis, giving my receipt back. *"It is yours."*

I read it. It was signed as Mayno. Everyone loses, sooner or later.

THE BOUNDARIES OF MYCENAE

The boundaries of Mycenae are strong, the Cyclopes have built them.

The legend tells that nobody, man or god, can demolish them.

They will be always standing, warning of power, of strength, bastions of the civilization.

The father of my father's father has seen Ilium, powerful, strong and rich. Nine years of war before returning, old and tired, to let him be murdered. But it was a necessary crime, at least as well as that proud and obstinate war. This way the wise men tell. Nine years in a tent, sleeping on the bare ground of a distant Country. Approach under the hostile boundaries to shake a bronze sword every day. Nine years for one day of looting. Who knows what he thought, what he dreamt in that tent. What strength has forced him to make war to so distant people; what has pushed him to such a long siege? The poets tell that this happened because of a queen, and they are perhaps right.

I cannot understand the reason that pushed my ancestors to such an insane enterprise. The best youth of Mycenae wore out in those lands. When the warriors came back home, the town was not the same anymore; it was transformed without soldiers. The fame of Mycenae scattered all over the world and the town became one hundred times richer; they forgot some uncomfortable and rough bronze brothers by now. Mycenae was changed, as all the cities change in the years. Talkative merchants, busy artisans, refined poets, elegant painters. The shepherds bargained over skins and wool with an expensive price. The treasure of any noble man, it was superior to the whole loot of that stupid war. And the warriors' faces, ingénue line only the faces of the warriors can be, hardened by the field and the ignorance, they looked surprised that foreigners, their painted armours, the liberty of their lovers, the wealth of their houses, the paintings. They poets tell that the warriors could not understand the new fashions; they also fought them with the sword. Coming back, they found different people.

What were Agamemnon's thoughts in front of those hostile boundaries? And what did he feel coming back home, when he discovered to have got old, to be an obstacle, with his broken sword? The father of my father's father fought that war. He got an armour like mine, made with this nice and shiny bronze. But it was not painted. All of our warriors have the bronze armours, shiny, well oiled. There are some gilded studs on mine, like Hector's ones, Priam's son that had my same rank. It seems I can see him, while he was spying from the slopes of his town that barbaric enemies, obstinately camped around and only God knows why. Barbarians waiting like crows that the man becomes simple flesh, and the town useless stones cooked by the sun. For years, every morning, that man leaned out from the slopes and looked in the eyes the father of my father's father, just like me, today, I look in the eyes the Barbarian that is out the boundaries and shakes that grey weapon, that invincible cutlass.

I don't know what my ancestor thought, crouched in the cold of the night, close to the boundaries of the hostile town, what he felt, what feelings, memoirs and prayers. I understand what Hector felt, his enemy. I know what his thoughts were, I can read the dismay in the folds of his face, I see the same show that his eyes saw, over the boundaries of Priam's town. The Barbarian would have come soon. He would have tried to climb towers to break down doors every day. He would have been rejected every day: but till when? I can read his thoughts like the clay tablets of the scribes that continue their job, while the Barbarians cast glances full of hate at us. A hate we don't know. If I could understand what pushed Agamemnon to the siege, I could perhaps save my town. But I don't understand.

I am not used to the armour. It is heavy. The Barbarians sing and speak a language I don't understand out there. I would like only to understand.

I don't understand this greed to destroy, this desire of blood and flames, the thirst of violence. The files, the sources, the rooms with the refined frescos, the columns decorated with scenes, the embroidered dresses, the painted amphora, they don't interest to the Doris.

The boundaries of Mycenae won't stop them.

SUMERIAN TABLE

"*A raged with the whole sky. Enlil instigated the air and the earth whirled with it. Enki lifted the fury of the waters. And the kingdom of Dumuzi, the plants, the fields, the woods: all destroyed. After the waters, the whole stock of Inanna cried (...) since earth became sterile like the abdomen of an old woman.*

Subir is a total downfall. Because your children are forced (...) like the shepherd? The downpour passed and the nomad came. Kiemgira went to ruin and the Barbarian pastures on the fields that were fertile and he eradicates the roots that are in Subir still. Why had I, the Ensi that regulates the flow of the waters, to assist to the punishment inflicted to the children of Kiemgira?

When the nomad has come, he has brought stronger swords and fierce anger, and he has destroyed the fields of the children of Kiemgira. Where is Gilgamesh Lord of Kullab? Why doesn't he come back to send away the enemy? Why does he allow that a sacrilegious foot climbs the steps of the sacred ziqqurat? Where is Lugalbanda, Lord of Uruk? Let's wait for Sipar that created the universe and defeated Imdugud, the bird of the storms that stole the Tables of the Destiny to the Gods, to have the power of dominion on the world. But king Sipar doesn't come. Even his son Dumuzi helps us, since this is the season in which he comes down to hell (...) the heat in the summer kills him every year. His bride Inanna is with him. Have all forgotten the land of Kiemgira and Sumerian people then?

Every night Nanna, Enlil's son, Nigal's bridegroom, crosses the sky on a boat in the form of scythe. But nobody assists the people from the weapons of the nomad. I am the Ensi, servant and celebrant of Utu that is the God of the light, custodian of the laws of Sumerians and supreme Judge. He dissipates the darkness and sees all what happens in the world. I, here in the bright temple, raise my prayer to him.

Oh Utu, Lord of the Sumerians land, men's father! When you go to rest, the world sleeps with you. And when you, young Utu wake up, the earth wakes up with you. If you are not there, no bird looks for its grain, and no man straight walks. You are nearby fraternally to the man walking alone!"

BLOSSO

I didn't believe Spartacus could have got it. I myself, accomplice of Tiberius Gracchus, paid the pirates since they carried the rebels to Africa. They would have joined to other rebels for the same cause from there. However, others paid the pirates for the opposite cause, and Spartacus died. And with him, thousands of men. Shortly after, also Tiberius would have died, murdered by the Senate of his town, he himself who was Tribune of it.

I didn't stand the disgust of that crime, and I came to Asia. You will wonder why to Pergamo. We, in Rome, knew well what and where the revolts of the populaces were against the tyrants. I am a philosopher, and I handle the sword. However, contrarily of many fellow citizens, I use my mind and not only to quote the lawyers of the Forum and the verses of the poets into favour. When the third Attalo left his Kingdom in Rome, it was not to see the populaces to triumph. Since Aristonico, his only son, just like Servio Tullio, was born by a slave who played the harp. He was not destined to the throne: he would have freed the slaves. Nevertheless, you cannot understand. The memory of the kings of Rome is accursed by the Senate. For this reason I am here, Publio Licinio Crassus. Just to remember who you are. Now I note in your eyes a "patrician" look, a sinister light. You that belong to one of the noblest families of Rome, you will know that the first patricians didn't possess ancient vases; they didn't admire refined paintings; they didn't flatter of fine wordings, and they didn't discuss about letters or philosophy. They had well other duties: the sow gives birth; the fields are thirsty, manure is scarce; the ox is hungry. Ah, noble Crassus, how different your people were! You have despised Eudo, Tiberius, Spartacus. However, in your crumbling *insulæ*, the rent immediately had to be paid. Aristonico has frightened the world and could unite Rome and all its enemies. How many legions are behind that sword? They have been enough for you, noble Consul, without the armies of Mitridate from Ponto, Nicomede from Bitinia, Ariate from Cappadocia, Pilemone from Paflagonia? So many kingdoms against a gang of servants. What an enterprise, Crassus! Come back to Rome, make the fetters of Aristonico triumph. Do you laugh, Crassus? Does this poor and philosopher man amuse you? However, you Crassus, you that laugh at other people's fate; you that have got a palace, that guide an army, do you believe yourself a patriot? Not the slaves, but the masters will destroy Rome: by the vice, the softness and the eases. Do you want to have a good time more? When the eagles of Rome won't fly anymore, unknown tribes of Barbarians will drag the fetters of the Senate. Does my agony amuse you? One day your soldiers, dragged in an insane enterprise, will see you wearing the toga, and they will understand there is no escape. Then you will remember my words, and you will know how to die, better than you have lived. Don't you laugh anymore Crassus? Are you superstitious? Then learn the lesson: you won't drag my fetters; you won't show me like a prey to other raiders. Since I don't handle this sword well, but contrarily of you, I know where to find my heart.

THIRTY SEVEN

There is something of my life which is escaping. Like the *"why am I here"*, now, in this place.

The sea. And this thievish destiny that has stolen my soul and dignity. And this number that persecutes me: thirty seven.

After all I would not like to come back. And I like thinking I can keep on living. Often, this dull and rhythmical noise, it helps me to think. Thinking. Thinking. Since thinking dissuades me from the work, it keeps me in contact with the universe. I have seen the sea for the first time when I was just twenty years old. I know all the stars one by one, so much that I could count them in my mind. Now that I am more than thirty years old, the sea keeps on being a mystery to me.

The thought of freedom of this sweep of endless water. The darkest night. The burning day. The storm. The fires turning around the masts of the ships. The lightning. The beauty of a storm. The mystery of the lightning. This mysterious messenger that strikes. And this number that persecutes me: thirty seven. Thirty seven years old, thirty seven men, thirty seven chickens, thirty seven fishes, thirty seven ships, thirty seven rows, thirty seven sails, thirty seven vases, thirty seven soldiers, thirty seven...

The rhythmical noise helps me to think. I think about home. I think to my nephews that are playing and to my sister calling them; she reproaches them because they don't obey. And I think about the mountains, the tops I have seen till now, they have inspired me poetries, songs... I like thinking I am flying above those white tops... Above the little ponds where the herds drink... Along the paths and the whirling streams. Flying like the eagle, seeing the hare and diving, grabbing it for fun... The hare escapes. Being the hare running on the lawn, fast. The buck in the wood browsing on the grass. Sometimes I dream to be a gull and plunge in the sea. I can feel the water of the sea, lukewarm. And I wet my wings, and I grab a fish. And this noise helps me to think, and I don't feel the work anymore. And this number that persecutes me.

-Thirty seven!

The head rows, I look at him.

-The commander wants you, upstairs - he says - Twenty-nine will replace you.

I get up, I don't believe it.

-Come one, before the head changes his mind. Twenty-nine! Come to the oar!

He got a lash too.

TIBERIUS
AND CAIUS

Caius observed the town from the Aventino hill. The Roman night was leaving, little by little, space to the vague light of the horizon that announced the imminent sun rising.

A rooster sang, announcing the dawn.

The man breathed deeply the prickly air of the morning.

-Caius- Tiberius, his brother, said -you don't hear me...

"How it is possible?" Caius Sempronius said to himself, *"The Senate doesn't hear that the sons of Rome, on whom the works of the job and war weigh, they are thirsty for justice? Were not ten years of war therefore, useful?"*

-Caius- Tiberius said -I have fought for this, ten years by now... It was thanks to my tenacity the agriculture reform was gotten. However, what price for this, do you remember? Ten years by now...

Caius observed the dawn, regardless of all surrounding him.

-Nobody could understand- Tiberius continued. Caius, impassive, stared the infinite, dipping himself in his own thoughts.

Tiberius deeply sighed.

-But how can you remember... You were just a little boy... How can you remember...

Caius was motionless, his staring look toward the town boundaries.

-And when my colleague Octavius put the veto, do you remember? The Meetings Tributes immediately dismissed him. I asked for the distribution of the Ager Publicus to the people without an income, and I got it. People of Rome had to have what it was up to them...

-My brother Tiberius made many noble things - Caius said in a low voice - I have so many things to say too.

-You believe too much in the people- Tiberius said -people shout... And when you find yourself with the people, on the battleground, while you need more help to get what themselves have the right, the poor man runs away; he hides; he even joins the enemies...

Caius shook his head, absorbed in his own thoughts.

The slave looked perplexed his master while he was speaking; he feared that the fading of echoes of the battle had upset his mind. He was a right man, Caius, and he had not to finish a correct struggle that way.

-But- Tiberius continued -when I have proposed that all the italic faithful to Rome got citizens, the noble people dragged the plebeians with them. I damaged their only privilege: the citizen of Rome. United, they shouted to the betrayal...

Caius turned toward the slave.

-The next request from Tiberius would have been the liberty for the slaves- he said.

The sharp declaration left the elderly servant stunned, and he was speechless. He knew Tiberius. That is, he knew him since he was a child.

-Yes- Tiberius said -I have meditated for a long time this idea...

-Look- Caius said to the slave -they are coming. They believe to defend their wealth: five hundred jugers of land. The wealth of hunger.

The slave, surprised more and more, listened to the words of his master.

-You cannot hear the voice of your brother- Tiberius said -you don't remember what happened when I tried to get Tribune for the second time, against every custom? Do you remember what happened to me? They will do the same to you. They speak about rights, about their rights. Nevertheless, don't touch their privileges. Since they love the privileges: and they have only a piece of land and the citizen of Rome.

Caius was observing the team at the feet of the hill.

-Runaway, Caius, before it is too late. Take the servants with you and the people who followed you. People will abandon you...

"If I ran away" Caius murmured to himself; *I would not be worthy of my brother Tiberius, and of the people that have followed me confident, with the faith in freedom, in equality. My people won't abandon me."*

-Count your friends Caius!- Tiberius with sad tone said -and count your enemies...

"And where I would go" Caius said to himself.

-...they all will stay to look...

Caius stayed an instant thoughtful, but he had decided for a long time already.

Caius turned to the slave and put the bracelet off from him: "Take me back to Caius" there was written there.

-Wait for me here- Caius said to him, getting further -anyway it goes, at least you will be free.

-People will believe that Caius has betrayed Rome...-Tiberius said.

The ghost of Tiberius, which nobody could see, slowly went away from the hill. The new freedman heard a rustle behind his shoulders and looked at the plants: there was no breath of wind. He felt a shiver. He turned toward the place from which the ghost was going away: he feared a trap, but he reassured, there was no one. Only trees...

THE DIVINE PROPHET

I am now dreaming. Here it is! A dream I could touch with my hand. I feel I will dream like only a great poet can. I will dream an epic dream, I want it! And I am an Emperor. I feel on me this aura of magic going down on the prophets alone; I hear the cries, the voices of an encircled building... It is marvellous. This dream is marvellous. I have always loved the song. The muse inspires me, but I need strong emotions. Ah! What a splendid dream I am having! I move along the rooms, men and servants run in every direction, as if the damned souls of their ancestors came back together all. And they shout and cry. Tearing their hair. Unworthy son of much Country! They are cowardly and ignoble even in a dream! There is also that idiot of the praetorian Beclezio: I cancel him, I don't like him. And then he has knelt and cries. How disgusting: I cancel this piece. Disappear, Beclezio! He has escaped away now. Well. When I wake up, I don't want to remember him. What a noise out there! Now I imagine a nice noise sounding like a crowd in terror... I want to dream... I want to dream a siege! I am the Divine Prophet and therefore I dream what I like. Now I go to the balcony, since I want to dream a real town, not mine. I have decided: I will dream Troy siege! Ah, I have always desired to dream Troy siege! As Homer dreamt it, who was poet, and therefore blind. Yes, yes! I already hear the howling crowd, the din of the fire, I hear the terror of their mothers, and I can touch with my hand the screeching of the flames devouring the town... And the soldiers sacking the houses... And the animals trying to break the chain! Oh, sublime muse! Give me the lyre! What a splendid dream. Here it is, I am dreaming a light, I now appearing at this window of Priam's palace: horror! Here it is the town that burns and the darkness breaks, it tears the dresses to the weeping mothers, the screeching of the flesh in the ardent furnace! Sing me oh goddess the anger of the Greeks and the infamous fury! Ah, what a show! Ah, powerful persons... I thank you very much for this dream inspiring my mind! Great, this Trojan people dying in the town of their own ancestors... I perceive the odour of the flesh that burns... The howling servants. And down there I see a soldier running! Ah, powerful persons, what a show you have granted me to see! Still a Phrygian staircase! Oh Calliope! Oh, Euterpe! Oh, numi! Troy burns and I, Nero Claudius, have no notes anymore!

THE AUSTRIAN

(Marie Antoinette)

Where have you sent me to die, mother? Which Country is mine? They try me as French for the simple reason not to be. My husband is dead, and my child has testified against me. Mother, why have not prepared me to this? You knew that one day I would have encircled a diadem and that my children would have had to reign. Where are my children now? And that hostile people of my cell wait only the passage of that cart that takes to the final action of this ridicule pamphlet. Great Empress, why have you not moved your Country to save me? Where is my brother-in-law with the long tongue, the Count of Provenza? Where is my beloved Fersen? Where are you? Cowardly poor men, where are you hidden? How many questions! Abbot de Vermond, you that had an answer to everything, where are you? Now that you should accept my confession, I have to bear the sight of a false priest who wants to know my secret to tell them to the world. I don't want a false priest. I want my children: where are my children?

TUATHA DE' DANANN

(Goddess Dan's people)

They say that in the Connacht there is a ghost. People of Ireland! What an imagination... I have been living in the Connacht for so long time, I don't remember the day when I came anymore.

They say the ghost plays the bagpipe when the sun is setting. I am playing instead, not the ghost. Eh! I have been crossing the heaths for a long time!

I remember a time in which, approaching to the houses, people let me come in, they gave me hospitality. Without knowing me, they harboured me and shared with me that little they had. And a bowl of beer never missed. In the evening, I played for them: it was great party and people sang and danced around the fire.

Well, I would not look a nostalgic man or some of those crying individuals on the beautiful gone times and they don't remember that one on three starved. No, no. I don't regret anything indeed! On the other hand, what should I regret? And then, I have got my friends. Next to Loch Glynn, in the county of Roscommon, the cobbler Luchorpain lives. He could tell so many things! He has been watching a hidden treasure for his whole life... Who could imagine that slender and little body hides a big energy? Yet anybody, neither man nor dragon, discovered the secret. I don't even know it. But it is probable that you didn't hear about it...

Have you ever seen the Puca? It is him that turns into a he-goat. Then it jokes with people: when he speaks, all believe that it is a spell... People of Ireland! Kelpie, loves instead the spectacular things, and it appears to the people with some witty remarks: he loves going out from the lakes or from the ponds with the shape of a horse.

Also "good people" are my friends. If meet one of them, be careful! They are not dangerous, they are all real jokers. They could joke with you very much. But the people of Ireland respect them, they love them.

You will wonder who I am. I am one like so many others; I play my bagpipe when the sun is setting. All those hearing me play, they are spellbound because (in all modesty) I am the best in the Connacht; rather, the best of the whole Erin! Because of this, people believe that a ghost is playing. I don't believe in ghosts. I have a long head!

You won't believe it, my guys, but I have known Mil's children coming here from Spain to produce the Celtics. There were only my people before and that foolish of the chaos: Balor with his malefic eye, for example. He was really a giant, one from Fomoire. Because I have seen seriously the giants.

I have also known Grainne Oigh. Have you ever heard about the virgin Grainne? The one recovering people; the princess of Munster, my guys. Saint woman, that one! And I bet my pipe that you have never heard about the *Coirte bovhan*, the carriage of the women of the *sidh* passing silent in the air...

Guys, word of honour, I have seen Dublin growing from when the heath was crossed by the Fiannas: it was called Baile Atha Cliath at that time! Fionn Mac Cumhaill has passed with his dog Bran and the gangs of warlike hunters, and Ireland was called Erin. I have been playing the bagpipe since then. So many years passed by from then, so may that you could not even count them. I have been playing for men and my people since time of the sun and the moon, since the time of the buck and the wild boar, since the time of the salamander: goddess Dan's people. That's why I smile when men of Ireland are afraid of the ghosts. I have a long head. Believe me guys, ghosts don't exist.

STORIES

Speech on man
The Doge of Venice
Grajano
Drink with me Publio Cornelio Scipione
The left-handed
The outlet of Deacon Paul
What are you saying stupid man?
The hunter
The grenadier
The emperor's soldiers
The boundaries of Mycenae
Sumerian table
Blosso
Thirty seven
Tiberius and Caius
The Divine Prophet
The Austrian
Thuatha de' Danann

Don't miss out!

Visit the website below and you can sign up to receive emails whenever Duilio Chiarle publishes a new book. There's no charge and no obligation.

https://books2read.com/r/B-A-RKNFD-LSARF

BOOKS 2 READ

Connecting independent readers to independent writers.

Did you love *The Doge of Venice and Other Stories*? Then you should read *IL MARCHIO*[1] by Duilio Chiarle!

Questa vicenda narra di ciò che accadde tra il 972/973 nel nord Italia e nel sud della Francia. Santi, monaci, guerrieri e semplice gente del popolo alle prese con uno dei periodi peggiori della storia d'Italia: il X secolo.

Read more at chiarleduilio.jimdo.com.

---

1. https://books2read.com/u/bzx5Bn

2. https://books2read.com/u/bzx5Bn

Also by Duilio Chiarle

Grandi poesie italiane

Le grandi poesie italiane - Antologia di grandi poeti da Dante a
Saba

Le grandi poesie italiane Volume 2

Amore mio - antologia di grandi poesie d'amore italiane

La grande letteratura italiana

Saggio storico su "Una partita a scacchi di Giuseppe Giacosa"

Le pasquinate ovvero la grande satira

Storie di Vino: Antologia di grandi Autori dal medioevo al '900

Storie di scacchi ovvero gli scacchi nella letteratura italiana – I
grandi autori italiani che hanno raccontato gli scacchi e la vita
quotidiana dal medioevo al novecento

Tre storie italiane di fantascienza: Settembrini, Nievo, Salgari

Storie di caffè ovvero il caffè nella letteratura italiana

Storie di formaggio ovvero il formaggio nella letteratura italiana

Storie di birra - antologia di grandi autori della letteratura
italiana

Storie di cioccolato - Antologia di grandi autori della letteratura italiana
Niente è come sembra: il culo nella letteratura italiana dal medioevo all'800
Storie di pipa ovvero la pipa nella letteratura italiana
Storie di guerra - Testimonianze dirette, dal medioevo alla prima guerra mondiale
Storie di gatti: i miei, i vostri, quelli raccontati dai grandi della letteratura italiana ovvero i gatti nella letteratura italiana dal medioevo al primo novecento

Storie della guerra fredda
La pelle del serpente

Standalone
Dieu li volt
Io sono Melody
La difesa Alekhine
Love Haiku
Paper Gods
The Doge of Venice and Other Stories
Domus aurea
Facezie, ovvero le barzellette di Leonardo da Vinci
Haiku d'amore
Dio è con Noi
Disarmony: Racconti Rosa "Sciocching"
Il Doge ed altre storie

La posta di Eustachio
Manuale di Giornalismo Investigativo
Meritokrazia
Oltre ogni Limite - Racconti ai Confini della realtà
I Naufraghi
Il Punto più Vicino al Cielo
Micronazioni: Storia dei più piccoli Paesi del Mondo
Gli dei di carta
L'Ultima Crociera
Scrittore fai da te: guida all'autopubblicazione
Ël Dòge e d'àutre stòrie
Jë dèi 'd carta - Comedia an unich at
I PAPI - i pontefici e le profezie papali di Malachia - storia e curiosità
Mistero e leggenda nove enigmi inestricabili dall'isola non trovata al caso Taman Shud
La pace - Storia e letteratura da Caino ai giorni nostri
Le figure del risorgimento senza risorgimentitori ovvero i personaggi del risorgimento visti dai loro contemporanei
Le notti buie dei Franchi
TG - Commedia breve in atto unico
Tg Piemont - Comedia brev an at unich
Tre uomini a spasso: la scienza non può spiegare tutto...
I giorni di Oceli
Capolinea Ferrero
Fruntac - Il signore delle folgori
Muramasa
MURAMASA
DREAMWEAVERS
IL MARCHIO

Watch for more at chiarleduilio.jimdo.com.

About the Author

Duilio Chiarle, writer and guitarist of "The Wimshurst's Machine".Duilio Chiarle, scrittore e chitarrista dei "The Wimshurst's Machine".Ha ricevuto il premio "Cesare Pavese" nel 1999. Gli sono stati attribuiti i premi internazionali "Jean Monnet" (patrocinato dalla Presidenza della Repubblica Italiana, dall'Università di Genova e dalle Ambasciate di Francia e Germania) e "Carrara - Hallstahammar" (quest'ultimo per due volte consecutive).Con il gruppo musicale "The Wimshurst's Machine" ha ricevuto tre nomination hollywoodiane consecutive: sono suoi i racconti dei "concept" musicali.Ha ricevuto l'onorificenza di "Ufficiale" dell'Ordine al Merito della Repubblica Italiana.

Read more at chiarleduilio.jimdo.com.